Torp the Dragon.

Stop that Owl!

Written and Illustrated by R. Butler

For Daniel x

Thank you to my wonderful children Jessica and James and to my family and friends.

Without your support and guidance, I would have never achieved this.

Special editors, D.B, R.G, J.G, M.G, C.G. The Ladies - A.M, E.B, N.A and N.D thank you all.

Other titles in this series.

Torp the Playful Little Dragon

Torp the Dragon – Stop that Owl!

More titles to follow…

www.torpthedragon.info

Text and illustrations copyright © 2015 R. Butler

First Printing: 2015

ISBN-13: 978-1512332087
ISBN-10: 1512332089

Butler Publishing

Swoosh! Torp the dragon loved to play and *Loop the Loop* was his favourite game. Swish! He would fly on the high winds, at great speeds with his best friends in tow, all cheering and waving. They would whizz around the church spire, hurtle through the clouds and skim the tops of the trees.

Playing with Torp was such fun. They had lots of favourite games.

Old Cat's favourite game was *Snow Sculptures*. Each of the friends would make a snow sculpture of themselves and then dress them up with hats and scarves.

Fox's favourite game was *Hide and Snow Seek*. Played on a snowy day, there always seemed to be extra places to hide. Can you see him?

Miss Mouse's favourite game was *Sticky Arrows*. Using lots of sticks, laid in arrow shapes she would create a treasure hunt. Everyone loved this game because the treasure at the end was always delicious!

It was while they were all playing Sticky Arrows that another adventure with Torp began. Fox knew they were getting close to the treasure because he could smell a tasty treat near by.

As he sniffed the air, his ears pricked up. Something had caught his attention.

"Run!" he suddenly yelled. "Run back to your homes, Grumpy Owl is back! Help! Help us Torp!"

As the little friends fled back to the safety of their homes, Torp leapt into the air and saw Grumpy Owl swooping silently down towards Miss Mouse's house.

"Stop that Owl!" she squeaked as she ran safely to her mouse house.

"Who goes there?" bellowed Torp.

Owl swooped down towards Old Cat. His sharp talons extended as if to grab him. However, instead of clawing at Cat, he grabbed Cat's mat instead! He stole it away into the air, leaving a scared but lucky Old Cat behind!

"Stop that Owl!" cried Old Cat.

For a moment, Owl had disappeared… Old Cat was most upset.

"My mat," he wailed, "Grumpy Owl has taken my best mat! Where am I going to sleep?" He gloomily pressed his paws into the bare ground where his cosy red mat used to be.

"I will never sleep soundly again!" he whimpered. "What shall I do?"

"What is that Grumpy Owl up to?" asked Torp.

Whoosh! Suddenly, Grumpy Owl flew back. He circled the churchyard and then headed over to Fox's patch. There was an almighty kerfuffle, as Fox barked and bins were knocked over. Torp flew over to help. He fired up his noisy sparklers and startled Grumpy Owl. He flew away, right over their heads, carrying Fox's empty box between his talons!

"Stop that Owl!" cried Fox.

"Why does Owl want Fox's box and Cat's mat? What is he up to? Let's go and see him on his ledge," insisted Torp. "Jump on my back Fox and hold tight!"

With a giant leap into the air, Torp swiftly carried Fox to the top of the tower.

There they found Grumpy Owl, twittering and flapping about.

"What are you up to, Owl?" asked Torp. "You are being unkind to my friends and you have taken things that do not belong to you."

"Oh bother!" grumbled Owl. "I do wish you'd leave me alone."

Fox spoke up bravely, "Leave you alone? **You** should leave **us** alone!"

"Why are you being so mean and grumpy?" asked Torp.

"I don't want to be grumpy. I just am…I wish I wasn't. I am running out of time to prepare my ledge for Mrs Owl's eggs. She will be arriving soon for springtime. I have been trying to fix it all year. It is too cold and damp."

Owl grumbled on…"I thought that Old Cat's mat and Fox's box would fix it."

"But you can't just take things that are not yours," said Torp. "Give these things back and let us help you."

"Can't! Shan't!" answered a stubborn, Grumpy Owl.

Torp fired up his sparklers. They crackled loudly, hurting Owl's ears.

"…Oh, all right then!" said a reluctant Owl, who then returned the mat to Cat and the box to Fox - who were very pleased to have them back!

The little friends had bravely gathered around Owl.

"Will you stop chasing us now?" asked Miss Mouse.

"Mice are supposed to be chased!" snapped Grumpy Owl.

Owl corrected himself; "Ahem… No, I won't be chasing you, besides I don't have time to, I *must* prepare a nest for Mrs Owl's arrival."

Torp suggested a trip to the woods to speak to the squirrels.

"I'm not asking *squirrels* for help!" Owl boasted proudly. He jumped to the ground and started pacing up and down. "Squirrels are like mice, they're there to be chased!"

Brave Miss Mouse stopped him in his tracks.

"Then we can't help you," she said. "The squirrels know all the best places for setting up a home. They are tree experts and can build the most amazing tree houses."

Owl had a think…he thought a tree house sounded rather splendid.

"Well…I suppose if I don't have to eat *this* mouse, I don't have to eat *those squirrels* either."

"We will fly together," said Torp. "Jump on my back and hold tight!"

Fox, Old Cat and Miss Mouse loved flying with Torp and this flight was going to be especially exciting with Owl following too. Across the hillside they flew, over the train bridge to the woods and the squirrel colony. However, no one was prepared for what happened next.

Owl couldn't help himself. He swooped down towards the squirrels chasing them back to their homes, causing utter chaos! A braver scurry of squirrels started hurling pinecones through the air and it quickly became pandemonium!

"What are you doing?" Torp called to Owl, "Stop it now!"

Owl really didn't mean to, it was in his nature. He landed on a branch near by to calm himself down.

"I'm sorry," sighed Owl, "I really didn't mean to!"

The entire wood fell silent.

Torp suggested that Owl should say sorry. Quick thinking Owl flew around the trees, picked nuts and acorns and started to deliver them to each of the squirrel houses. It was his little way of saying sorry.

One by one the squirrels popped their heads out of their houses, to enjoy the feast of nuts and acorns.

"Owl isn't here to chase you," Torp said to the squirrels. "He has come for your help. Please can you help him find a new home for Mrs Owl? If you would be so kind, he will make sure he delivers fresh nuts and acorns, every week."

The little squirrels had enjoyed their feast and agreed to take Torp, Owl and the little friends to a tree, at the edge of the woods. It was a very old tree with a perfect hidey-hole, right in the heart of the trunk. It felt cosy and dry. Mrs Owl would love it!

Owl kept his promise and thanked the squirrels with weekly deliveries of nuts and acorns.

When Mrs Owl arrived, the new home in the wood was a lovely surprise and soon after settling in, a clutch of beautiful owl eggs was laid.

When hatching time approached, Torp, Old Cat, Fox and Miss Mouse camped at the train bridge nearby, waiting for news of the baby owls. Camping here was very exciting, especially when a train went past! Whoooosh! Clickety clack, clickety clack!

Then, one sunny spring morning, Mr and Mrs Owl could be heard hooting across the meadow. It was the sign they had all been waiting for. The eggs were hatching. What a wonderful sight it was!

"Congratulations!" said Torp to Owl.

"What adorable hatchlings you have," squeaked Miss Mouse.

"Eggcellent!" joked Fox.

"Puuurfect," chuckled Old Cat.

Owl was so happy, "Thank you friends, thank you family." he replied.

They had a lovely time getting to know the baby owls. Of course they played lots of games. *Early Bird Catches the Worm* and *Sleeping Owls* were the best games for the little hatchlings. But it was actually Owl who had the most fun, playing with his new family and friends – he was no longer grumpy, in fact, he was the happiest Owl in the whole wide woods!

Reading activities to draw, write or discuss.

Each of the characters had a favourite game. Who liked to play *Sticky Arrows* and how do you play it?

What is your favourite game? What are the rules? Can you write instructions for your game?

Why did Owl upset every one at the start of the story?

What things make you feel grumpy?

Can you explain why Owl wanted to chase mice and squirrels?

How did Owl say sorry to the squirrels?

What is your favourite picture?

Do you know any other stories about animals?

Look at Torp's map on p30. Where would you like to play with Torp?

Draw a map of all your favourite places.

Torp's Map of the Hillside.

18800431R00021

Printed in Poland
by Amazon Fulfillment
Poland Sp. z o.o., Wrocław